I CAN DO IT BY MYSELF

by Lessie Jones Little
and Eloise Greenfield

Illustrated by Carole Byard

Thomas Y. Crowell Company   New York

By Eloise Greenfield

Rosa Parks

Sister

Paul Robeson

Me and Neesie

First Pink Light

Mary McLeod Bethune

Africa Dream

Honey, I Love

Library of Congress Cataloging in Publication Data
Little, Lessie Jones. I can do it by myself.
SUMMARY: Donny is determined to buy his mother's birthday
present all by himself, but he meets a scary challenge on the way home.
[1. Birthdays—Fiction] I. Greenfield, Eloise, joint author.
II. Byard, Carole M. III. Title. PZ7.L7228Iac [E] 77-11554
ISBN 0-690-01369-8 ISBN 0-690-03851-8 lib. bdg.

1 2 3 4 5 6 7 8 9 10

To my beloved husband and sweetheart, Weston W. Little, Sr., who has been a protecting rock — loving, dependable, and strong — and a wonderful father to our five children.

— Lessie Jones Little

To McKinley and Mildred Greenfield, for their quiet affection and for all the love they gave to help my children grow up.

— Eloise Greenfield

Donny felt the warm red sunshine on his eyelids and opened his eyes. He rolled slowly off the bed and made as much noise as he could falling on the floor.

"Ow!" he said loudly, but Wade, sleeping in the top bunk, didn't even move. If he would wake up, they could have some fun, but Donny knew better than to shake him or hit him with the pillow.

Then Donny saw his wallet right where he had put it before he went to bed, in the chair on top of his clean clothes, and he remembered what day it was. It was his mother's birthday. He was glad now that Wade was still asleep.

Donny went in the bathroom and splashed water on his face and wiped it with his towel. He didn't have time for all that washing up this morning. He had something important to do.

He hoped nobody had bought the plant. The big one with the waxy, green leaves and the little flowers that hung down like bells. Pink as strawberry ice cream. Mr. Haynes had promised to sell it to him for a dollar, if nobody had bought it by today. Donny smiled to himself, thinking about how surprised his mother was going to be when he brought it home.

He went back to his room and got dressed as quietly as he could. He rolled the legs of his too-long pajamas up to his knees and put his jeans on top of them. He combed his hair and put his wallet in his pocket, and he was all ready.

Then, while he was standing in front of the long

mirror, liking the way he looked, and practicing how he was going to stand cool when he paid for the plant, and how he was going to smile with his mouth closed so nobody could see that two teeth were missing, he looked up in the corner of the mirror and saw Wade's eyes. Wade was wide awake and laughing at him.

"You think you bad, don't you?" Wade said.

Donny couldn't think of anything smart to say back, and he wanted to make his brother stop laughing, so he took his wallet out of his pocket, opened it, and looked at his dollar.

"You going to get the plant!" Wade said.

"Yeah," Donny said. He put the wallet back in his pocket and gave it a cool pat.

"Wait for me," Wade said, climbing down the ladder. "I'm going, too."

"No, you not!" Donny said. He forgot all about being cool. "You can't go!"

"I have to help you," Wade said. "You know you too little to carry that big plant."

"I'm not too little," Donny said. "I can do it by myself." He gave Wade his meanest look before he started downstairs.

He felt mean, too. Big people always wanted to help you. They always wanted to explain things to you and do things for you, as if they could do everything in the world just because they were big. And big brothers were worse than anybody.

When he got downstairs, his mother was bringing the newspaper in from the porch.

"Hi, Donny," she said.

Donny said, "Hi," but he didn't stop.

"What's the matter?" his mother asked. "You're not giving out kisses this morning?"

"I don't have time," Donny said. He walked on down to the basement and got his wagon out from behind the washing machine. He liked that old wagon even if it did have a bent-up handle. It had belonged to his father when he was a little boy, and his father had left it for him when he moved away.

Donny pulled the wagon bumping and squeaking up the steps. When he got upstairs, Wade was standing there in his bathrobe, and his mother had her hands over her ears.

"Where you going with that thing?" his mother asked.

"I have to go somewhere, Mama," Donny said, talking fast. "And it's just around two corners, and I don't have to cross any streets, and I'll be right back in a minute."

His mother looked scared like she thought he was a little baby going off to get killed or something.

"Hey, Ma," Wade said, "how come Donny got fat knees?"

His mother didn't look at his knees. She said, "All right, Donny, go ahead. But you come right back now, you hear?"

She and Wade followed him to the door and watched him leave. "Can't you just tell me where you're going?" his mother called after him, but he didn't turn around.

Then Wade had to open his mouth and say something, too. Wade said, *"Hope that big ugly bulldog don't get you!"*

Donny felt funny in his stomach. He had forgotten all about that bulldog. He wished that he had gone the other way, the long way, but he couldn't turn around

now and let Wade laugh at him for being scared. He had to keep on going.

He turned the corner and met two ladies coming toward him. He smiled with his mouth closed and they smiled back, and then he heard one of them say, "Now,

ain't that the cutest little thing?" And right away he
stopped smiling.

He didn't smile at the man jogging in his sweat suit,
but the man stopped anyway. "You're not lost, are you,
sonny?" he said.

Donny didn't stop; he just shook his head. He wished
the wagon didn't squeak so loud. It sounded extra loud
now that he was getting near the yard where the dog
lived. He could see the dog beside his little house,
eating out of his silver pan, and he hoped the food was
too good to stop eating.

But the dog jerked his head toward the sound of the wagon and came running up to the fence barking loud and making terrible faces.

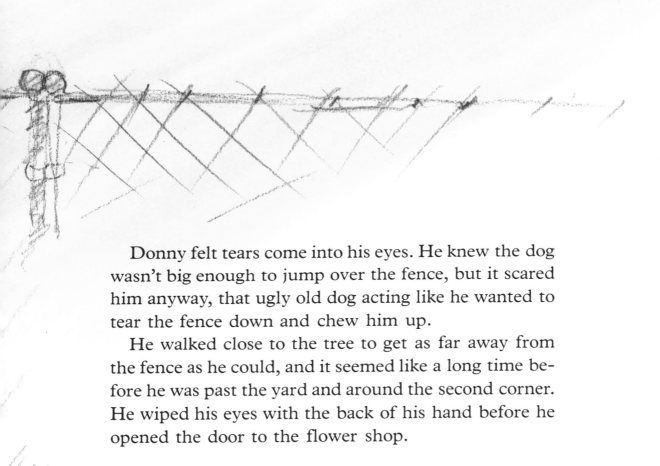

Donny felt tears come into his eyes. He knew the dog wasn't big enough to jump over the fence, but it scared him anyway, that ugly old dog acting like he wanted to tear the fence down and chew him up.

He walked close to the tree to get as far away from the fence as he could, and it seemed like a long time before he was past the yard and around the second corner. He wiped his eyes with the back of his hand before he opened the door to the flower shop.

His plant was still there, still standing on the end of the long table in the middle of the room. He looked around and didn't see Mr. Haynes, but that old Freddy was there, dusting the counter.

"What you want, kid?" Freddy asked. That Freddy was always trying to act like a man, and he wasn't much bigger than Wade.

Donny spread his feet a little apart and stuck his hands in his back pockets. He tilted his head to one side so he wouldn't have to open his eyes wide to look at Freddy.

"Who you calling a kid?" he said.

Freddy laughed. "You, kid," he said. "I'm calling you a kid."

Mr. Haynes came in from the back room, patting the sweat from the edges of his gray hair. He gave Freddy a look that put him back to work, then turned to Donny.

"Good morning," he said. "May I help you?"

"I want to buy a plant," Donny said. Mr. Haynes knew how to treat a customer. Not like some people. Mr. Haynes knew this wasn't like when he came in with Wade just to talk and hang around. This was business.

"Any special kind of plant?" Mr. Haynes asked.

Donny put a frown on his face. "I have to look around first," he said.

He walked around the table, looking at all the plants, until he came to the one with the strawberry ice-cream bells. "I want to buy this one," he said. "How much does it cost?"

"You're in luck," Mr. Haynes said. "It's on sale today for a dollar."

Donny took out his dollar and paid Mr. Haynes and put the receipt Mr. Haynes gave him in his pocket. Mr. Haynes put the plant in the wagon and walked him to the door. "Come in again," Mr. Haynes said.

"Okay," Donny said. "I'll come in again."

As soon as he got outside, Donny started smiling. He felt good pulling along the wagon with the plant that he had bought for his mother all by himself. He felt big, and he was walking and laughing and not caring about his missing teeth when he saw that the gate to the dog's yard was open. At the same moment, he heard a loud bark right beside him, and he knew it was the bulldog.

"Mama!" Donny said, and the dog barked again. Donny didn't know what to do. He wanted to turn around and run back to the flower shop, but he knew better than to run from a dog. He looked at the dog and the dog looked at him. "Mama!" he said again.

He wanted his mother, and he wanted his father, and he wanted all the people who had called him cute and sonny and kid, and he even wanted Wade. He didn't want to do anything by himself.

Donny began to cry, but he made himself keep walking. He walked backward so he could watch the dog. He cried and backed up, and cried and backed up some more, and he backed right into the tree and fell down. He fell, and the plant fell over in the wagon, but the dog just stood there looking, as if he were wondering why Donny was lying down there in the dirt. Then he gave a little bark, and walked back into the yard and lay down in the sun with his back to the fence.

Donny lay there for a minute, sniffling.

Then he got up, stood the plant up in the wagon, and wiped the tears off his face. He didn't feel big any-more. He felt like a baby. He could feel the dirt on his face, and his ear hurt where he had bumped it on the tree, and his pajama legs had come unrolled and were dragging on the ground. He felt just like a big old baby. Then he remembered that, even though he had been scared, he hadn't run. And when he remembered that, he felt better. He went over to the yard, closed the gate and latched it, and stuck out his tongue at the dog's back. And then he started home.

Donny pulled the wagon up to his front steps and called his mother.

"Hey, Mama!" he yelled. "Happy birthday! I got a surprise for you!"

His mother and Wade got to the porch before he finished calling. His mother had a funny look on her face, as if she were going to hug him right there, outdoors, but she didn't. She hugged the plant instead. She didn't say anything about the flowers that had fallen off. She just smiled, and even Wade was smiling.

"Thank you, Donald," his mother said. "It's a beautiful plant."

After she had taken it in the house, Donny just stood there on the porch and looked at Wade. Then he spread his feet a little apart, put his hands in his back pockets, and tilted his head to one side.

"See?" he said. "I told you I could do it by myself." He felt a big smile coming and he couldn't stop it, so he put his top teeth over his bottom lip to keep it from smiling too much.

About the Authors

Lessie Jones Little, a former schoolteacher in North Carolina, moved to Washington, D.C., in 1929 where she still lives with her husband, Weston W. Little, Sr. She is the mother of two sons and three daughters, a grandmother, and great-grandmother. Mrs. Little began writing in 1974 at the age of sixty-seven. This is her first published work.

Eloise Greenfield is the award-winning author of many children's books, including *Paul Robeson,* which won the 1976 Jane Addams Children's Book Award. Mrs. Greenfield is the daughter of Lessie Jones Little. Her childhood memories are dotted with images of "Mama being Mama"—gathering the neighborhood children into clubs and choirs, presenting programs and fashion shows. The collaboration for *I Can Do It By Myself,* Mrs. Greenfield says, is "one of the highlights of my life." She and her husband, Bob, live in Washington, D.C.

About the Artist

Carole Byard, a painter and a teacher of painting and drawing, has illustrated several picture books, including Eloise Greenfield's *Africa Dream.* She also does illustrations for magazines. Ms. Byard was born and grew up in Atlantic City, New Jersey. Since studying at the New York Phoenix School of Design, she has lived in New York City.

1827

E   Little, Lessie Jones
LIT

I can do it by
   myself

DATE			

© THE BAKER & TAYLOR CO.